The Wright Brothers' Flyer I (U.S.A.)—the first successful airplane

Sopwith F.1 Camel (U.

Fokker Dr. I (Germany)—
the Red Baron's plane

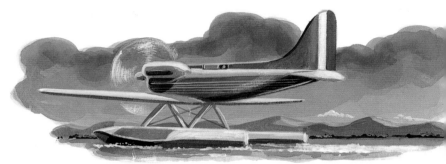

Supermarine S6B seaplane (U.K.)
1931 Schneider Trophy win

Blériot XI (France)

an NYP, *Spirit of St. Louis* (U.S.A.)—
arles Lindbergh's plane

Gee Bee R-2 (U.S.A.)

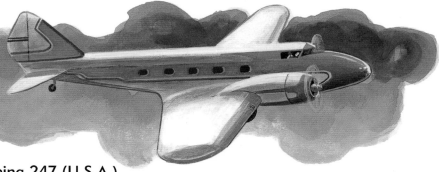

eing 247 (U.S.A.)

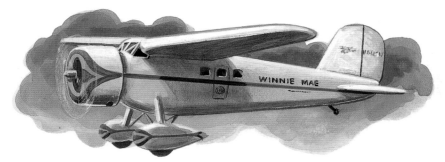

Lockheed Vega *Winnie Mae* (U.S.A.)

Ford 4-AT Tri-Motor (U.S.A.)

THIS PLANE

Paul Collicutt

A Sunburst Book • Farrar Straus Giroux

This book is for Charlie and Harry from Uncle Paul

Library of Congress Cataloging-in-Publication Data
Collicutt, Paul.
    This plane / Paul Collicutt.—1st ed.
        p.   cm.
    Summary: Simple text and illustrations present different types of airplanes
and the work they do.
    ISBN 0-374-47517-2 (pbk.)
    1. Airplanes—Juvenile literature. [1. Airplanes.] I. Title.
TL547.C54   2000
629.133´34—dc21
                                                                            99-26693

This plane is made of paper.

This plane is made of wood and canvas.

This plane is made of metal.

This plane is a biplane.

This plane is a triplane.

This plane taxis along a runway.

This plane taxis over water.

This plane takes off with a cata

This plane takes off vertically.

This plane carries passengers.

This plane carries cargo.

This plane gets fuel on the ground.

This plane gets fuel in the air.

This plane has propellers.

This plane has jet engines.

This plane is slow.

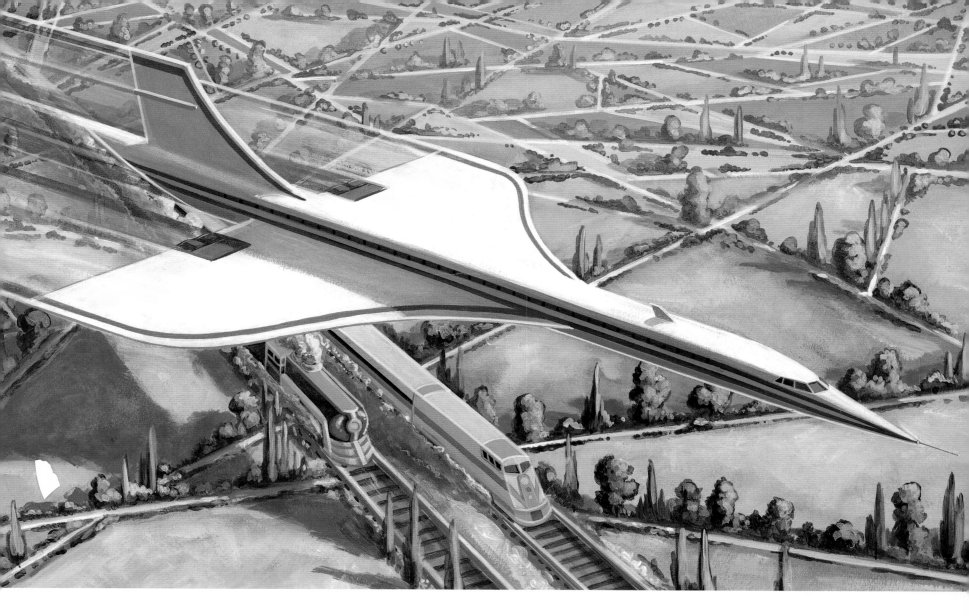

This plane is fast.

This plane leaves messages.

This plane picks up messages.

This plane drops supplies.

This plane drops water.

This plane has lowered its landing gear,

ready for touchdown.

Supermarine Spitfire (U.K.)

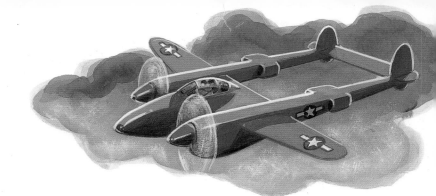

Lockheed P-38 Lightning (U.S.

Lockheed Super Constellation
(U.S.A.)

North American X-15 (U.S.A.
official record breaker for speed and heig

Boeing 314 flying boat (U.S.A.)

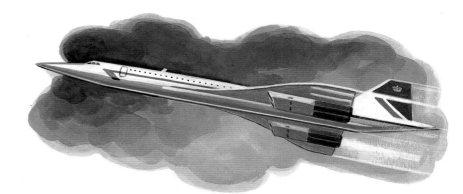

1 X-1 (U.S.A.)—first airplane to break the sound barrier

Aérospatiale/BAC Concorde (France / U.K.)—
first supersonic passenger plane

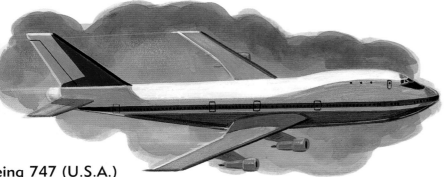

eing 747 (U.S.A.)

Hawker Siddeley Harrier (U.K.)

Douglas DC-3 Dakota (U.S.A.)